A Rainbow of Friends

Also by P. K. Hallinan

That's What a Friend Is!
Heartprints
How Do I Love You?
I'm Thankful Each Day!
Thank You, God
A Love Letter from God
Let's Be Thankful
Let's Be Friends
The Looking Book

P. K. Hallinan

A Rainbow of Friends

WORTHY®
kids

ISBN: 978-0-8249-5519-9

WorthyKids
Hachette Book Group
1290 Avenue of the Americas
New York, NY 10104

WorthyKids is a registered trademark
of Hachette Book Group, Inc.
Color separations by Precision Color Graphics,
Franklin, Wisconsin

Library of Congress CIP data on file

Designed by Georgina Chidlow

Printed and bound in U.S.A.
CW
25 24 23 22 21 20 19

This book is for

_____

From

_____

A rainbow of friends
is the vision we see
when we think about peace
and world harmony.

Some friends are funny.

Some friends are stars.

Some friends wear clothing that's different than ours.

A friend may be challenged
in movement or speech.

A friend may be distant or difficult to reach.

Still, each friend is given
a share of our hearts,
so no one feels different,
unloved, or apart.

A rainbow of friends
is a chance for us all
to help one another
when we stumble or fall.

We all have our interests.

We all have our views.

We all have our strengths
and our weaknesses too.

And though we may wander
a bit wide or far,
our friends still accept us
the way that we are.

A rainbow of friends
is a bonding together
that eases our journey
through all kinds of weather.

If we work hand in hand,
all jobs can be done.

If we play as a team,
we've already won.

Our goals can be reached with the greatest success by trusting that others are doing their best.

So reach out with love
to the people you meet,
and offer a smile
to all those you greet.

The world is a family
whose happiness depends
on a circle of caring . . .

on a rainbow of friends.